ALAN CARTER

LAST OUT OF BURMA

Collins

LONDON AND GLASGOW

First published 1967

© Wm. Collins Sons & Co., Ltd. 1967

PRINTED AND MADE IN GREAT BRITAIN BY
WM. COLLINS SONS AND CO. LTD.
LONDON AND GLASGOW

CONTENTS

1. The Bridge Busters

THERE WAS half an hour of twilight after
the sun set, then suddenly the jungle was
wrapped in thick, velvety blackness. A faint
pink glow far away in the south marked
where the retreating army of British and
Indian troops had fired the oil wells three
days earlier to prevent them falling into
Japanese hands. The fires were still raging.

All through that long hot day tired troops,
many of them wounded, had streamed over
the hundred-yard long bridge. Now they
were thinning out, and the sound of firing
was growing louder. The rearguard was
stubbornly holding back the crack units of
the 84th Japanese Infantry Brigade to give
those who could walk a chance to cross the
vital bridge.

On the north bank four men of the Royal
Engineers were finishing a scratch meal.
Captain Johnson's face had the strained look
of a man who has spent weeks shuttling back

and forth, mining a bridge, letting the army pass over, then destroying the bridge before racing on to prepare the next bridge for demolition.

His sergeant, Taffy Morris, lit a cigarette then held it out so that Sapper Hooky Walker could light one. Then Walker gave a light to young Jimmy Leach, also a sapper. In the light of the match all four looked as yellow as the dust which clogged the road. Weary feet had kept the air filled with dust all day. There was no getting away from it. It settled on eyebrows, eyelashes, lips, and caked with the sweat on cheek and brow.

It was fairly quiet now, for only the quiet murmur of the river and the sound of one or two people shuffling across the bridge broke the silence. They were the last pitiful remnants of the refugees: Burmese men, women and children fleeing from the cruel invader. Next would be the rearguard. When they were over, Captain Johnson would ram down the handle of the innocent-looking brown box, and the electric current generated would spark off the detonators attached to the slabs of guncotton which he and his men had fastened to each of the bridge piers. That would be that. The bridge would fall into the river, and another few valuable hours would be gained for the retreating army.

For close on an hour the bridge was deserted. The last refugee had come across and the only sounds came from the river and the jungle. The water rippled and made soft music. From the darkness of the jungle came the chatter of cicadas, beetle-like insects which never seemed to stop their endless calling.

Then the moon came up above the treetops. It shed a pale, mysterious light over the scene and Hooky Walker, a mountain of a man, looked up and whispered: " Gimme the moon, gimme a girl, and leave the rest to me."

Nobody laughed. Nerves were too strained. Some time ago the firing to the south had died down. All four knew what it meant. The weary rearguard were withdrawing. Soon there would be the clatter of nailed boots on the bridge as the men who had been holding up the Japanese advance, came racing across.

This time, however, before anyone set foot on the bridge, there was a thin, high-pitched whistle in the air above, and a few moments later a mortar shell exploded not more than thirty yards from where the four Engineers were crouched. They ducked, then slid into the slit trench they had dug earlier.

"This is going to be dicy, Sergeant," Captain Johnson muttered. "If they've got ahead of our fellows we may have to blow the bridge and leave the rearguard on the wrong bank."

"Yeah, it looks as if the yellow devils have outflanked our lads," Sergeant Morris agreed. "We . . . look out!" and he tried to get even lower in the trench as a second mortar shell whined towards them, to explode some twenty yards beyond, shattering a palm tree and starting a small fire in the undergrowth.

"Get that fire out, lads," Captain Johnson

urged. "It's bad enough with the moon, but if we have a fire lighting things up, our chaps won't stand a chance with the Japs in the undergrowth. They must have got pretty close to be able to use mortars on us."

"They're looking for us four," the sergeant suggested. "Blot us out and they keep the bridge. If . . ."

"Get that fire out!" Captain Johnson interrupted, "then get back here as quick as you can."

Morris, Hooky Walker and young Leach, bending low the moment they were out of the trench, scurried across to where the dry undergrowth was beginning to burn fiercely. It crackled alarmingly, flames shooting up over an area of several square yards.

The three Britishers stamped on the flames, and their boots were so worn with the long trek northwards from Rangoon that they could feel the heat through the wafer-thin leather. There was sufficient water flowing down the nearby river to put out a thousand such fires, but there was not time to carry it, even if they had possessed buckets.

At the end of ten minutes the last little licking flames were gone, and the three Britishers wiped their sweat-dappled faces. Only then did they realise that the firing had broken out again, and men were crossing the bridge.

"They are ours," Sergeant Morris said. "The Nips don't wear ammunition boots."

"I think they should make a rule to stop 'em wearin' these flippin rubber and canvas boots, Sarge," Hooky Walker snorted. "The yellow hounds can be on you before you know where you are, wearin' them sneakers. Why don't they wear proper boots?"

"Come on, don't stand there yapping," Sergeant Morris snarled. "Back to the bridge."

Even as they got to their slit trench there was a sudden tac-a-tac-taca-taca-taca-tac-tac from the undergrowth about eighty yards to the west of the bridge. The advance units of the Japanese army had arrived.

The clump-clump of boots on the bridge stopped at once. Men who had been fighting all the way up Burma acted instinctively when under fire. Down they went, hugging the dusty roadway of the bridge. Not one man returned the Japanese fire.

The gun, a Japanese *Nambu*, firing .256 ammunition stopped, fired two more short bursts, then was silent for a minute. The gun crew were sitting listening, waiting for the first whisper of sound which would tell them the men trapped on the bridge were starting to move again.

"If they move now that stinkin' machine-gun crew will get the lot," Sergeant Morris muttered. "If I were . . . oh, strike a light!" The exclamation of disgust was torn from him by the clump-clump-clump of boots on the bridge. At once the machine-gun opened up again, its position revealed by the rapid winking flashes of fire from its muzzle.

There was one twenty second burst, then came a different sound. The sharp cracking noise made when a hand grenade explodes. The staccato rattle of the machine-gun stopped, and from near the spot came a bellow:

"Okay, lads, get moving!"

"What were you sayin', Sarge?" Hooky Walker asked, a chuckle in his voice. "If they move that Jap gun would get the lot? He ain't got any." Nor had there been any casualties. The men on the bridge were all on their feet again, and a grinning sergeant in the lead was hooking a grenade back on his belt. It was the grenade being banged on the bridge boarding which had sounded like a man running, and made the Japanese machine-gun crew open up—an act which gave away their position to the three men who had gone down to winkle them out. It had needed only one grenade to do the "winkling."

There was a steady stream of men crossing the bridge now, and from the jungle came muffled explosions. The rearguard were not letting the triumphant Japanese get too close, and the booby traps they had left were taking a heavy toll of their pursuers.

There was, however, an increase in the number of mortar shells coming over; but desperately anxious not to damage the bridge, the Japanese were careful to drop their mortar shells on each side, and on the road beyond.

They were crossing now in a steady stream . . .

The last of the Gloucesters were coming over, with their C.O. bringing up the rear, when another Japanese machine-gun unit opened up from the east side of the bridge. The C.O. went down with a bullet through his leg, and knowing there was a unit of Engineers waiting to destroy the bridge he lifted himself on one elbow to bellow:

"Okay, Engineers, give it the works. I'm the last one."

For perhaps twenty seconds the fate of the rearguard hung in the balance. Captain Johnson hesitated over the plunger handle. To destroy the bridge now meant killing the Gloucesters' C.O. Yet by the wan light of the moon the little squad of Engineers saw men racing madly across the bridge. They were Japanese infantrymen, risking their lives to prevent the bridge being destroyed.

The machine-gun which had been raking the bridge with its deadly fire, stopped, and for seconds the night was quiet, quiet save for the pad-pad-pad of rubber-shod feet. Then Jimmy Leach jumped out of the slit trench, yelling:

"Hold it a second, sir."

As he ran he swung his right arm and a grenade sang through the air. It struck the bridge just ahead of the advancing Japanese. There were screams and howls as the pieces of hot grenade exploded. Seconds later Jimmy's remaining grenade burst, and pieces of hot metal sprayed the bridge.

Jimmy reached the Gloucesters' C.O. He grabbed him by the shoulders and dragged him backwards towards the bank. Then the machine-gun opened up again, the .256 calibre bullets pattering into the woodwork, or screaming off into the night as they ricocheted from an iron bolt.

Three of the Gloucesters had turned back, and they grabbed their C.O. just as Jimmy Leach got him off the bridge.

"Ta, chum," one of the Gloucesters yelled, and they galloped away into the darkness, dragging their C.O. along, his boot heels raising twin streams of dust. A moment later Captain Johnson rammed down the plunger of the galvanometer. An electrical impulse went through the unseen wiring to primers and detonators affixed to the slabs of guncotton lodged securely under each bridge pillar.

Balls of orange-yellow fire mushroomed to life. They revealed the bridge for a moment, with vague figures of Japanese soldiers racing back the way they had come. Then, as the air quivered with the roar of high explosives, the four sections of bridge fell with a tremendous splash into the river.

Wooden baulks, twisted ironwork, planking and other debris sang through the air before either falling into the river or crashing on to the banks. Then the machine-gun which had brought down the Gloucesters' C.O. opened up again.

It was joined by another, heavier machine-gun, and the two weapons raked the banks on either side of the bridge for almost ten minutes. When they stopped, a mortar came into action, and forced Captain Johnson, Sergeant Morris and Hooky Walker to keep down in their slit trench. The firing went on for almost half an hour.

"The cuckoos," Walker said after a minute or two. "As if we wouldn't have funkholes. Wastin' ammo, that's what they're doing."

Neither Captain Johnson nor Sergeant Morris made any comment. They knew the reason for this barrage. The Japanese would be trying to get men across the river, in an attempt to gain a foothold before the British could dig in. The fury of the rearguard action fought by the Gloucesters had deceived the Japanese into thinking the British were not so tired as they actually were.

Suddenly the firing died down. The first dozen men attempting to cross the river in the dark had found the going too tough, and the Japanese commander reluctantly decided to rest his troops while a temporary bridge was built.

"Think it's safe to go, Sergeant?" Captain Johnson asked, after a minute or so of nerve-shaking silence. "I don't think they've got any across, do you?"

"No, sir. I think they're calling it a day," Sergeant Morris said. "I think we should scarper . . . er . . . retire, now. If we can get to the car we can get to the next bridge by dawn . . . and maybe get an hour's sleep before starting on that."

"Right. Ready, Walker?" Captain Johnson asked, turning to Hooky.

"What about Jimmy, sir . . . er . . . Private Leach?"

"Oh, lor, yes," in the excitement of the past minutes Jimmy Leach had been overlooked.

"I'll get him, sir," Hooky said, and big man though he was, standing over six feet and weighing, before the forced march from Rangoon, nearly seventeen stones, he crawled slowly out of the slit trench and went smoothly over the ground like a monstrous snake across to the bridge-head.

The moon was well up now, and by its wan light it seemed impossible that the men on the other bank would fail to see Walker. From their trench Captain Johnson and Sergeant Morris waited, tense and expectant. They were waiting for the first twinkling jets of flame, to be followed at once by the crackle of a machine-gun.

Something splashed in midstream. It was

a girder which had been dangling by a stripped bolt, and had swung itself free. The two Britishers ducked, but nothing else happened.

They saw Walker reach the inanimate bundle which was Jimmy Leach.

" The fool . . . what's he standing up for?" Captain Johnson groaned, and again waited for the blasting hail of bullets. Day after day of demolition work, with the Japanese hard on his heels most of the time, had strained Captain Johnson almost to breaking point.

Hooky Walker was not troubled with nerves. In civilian life he was a coalman, his beefy frame being just right for handling hundredweight bags of coal. He never worried, and in a situation like this never gave a thought to what would happen if a Japanese gunner saw him.

He heaved Jimmy Leach across one shoulder, then began to stride up the road, the thick layer of yellow dust deadening the sound of his footsteps. Captain Johnson and Sergeant Morris, who was carrying the precious galvonometer, followed him.

Catching up to Hooky, Captain Johnson asked:

"Is he alive, Walker?"

"Dunno, sir; but we couldn't leave him there, could we? Shall I carry him round the bend in the road—in case the Nips open up again?"

"Yes, and keep to the side of the road. There's less chance of you making any noise there."

They hurried up the dusty road. It was pot-holed, and even in the moonlight it was possible to see the pathetic little objects, which the refugees had been unable to carry, lying here and there. There were also sidepacks and other items of equipment dropped by men of the Burma Rifles trying to lighten their load as much as possible during the retreat.

After about a hundred yards even Hooky was grunting under his burden, and Sergeant Morris took over from him.

"Strike a light," he grunted as the limp form of Leach was slid across his shoulder. "What's he got in his pockets? He feels as if he's stuffed with lead, and . . ."

"Quiet, quiet!" Captain Johnson ordered. "We should be getting near the car, and I don't want Harrison opening up on us."

Corporal Harrison stepped out of the shadows of the jungle a minute later when, by the light of the moon, he recognised Hooky's lumbering figure.

"There's no car, sir," he said, saluting, and before Captain Johnson could catch his breath, went on: "It was the Gloucesters, sir. They commandeered it. Their C.O. had a leg wound, and . . ."

"Commandeered *our* car," Captain Johnson said irritably. "Didn't you tell them that we are a priority, and . . ."

"I started, sir," Harrison said ruefully, "and one of their lads promised me a thick ear if I didn't get out of the car. They weren't in the mood for arguing."

"Somebody will be court-martialled for this," Captain Johnson spluttered. "We're due at Chaukyi bridge by dawn and . . . oh, well, come on. We'd better get moving or the Japs will have us. You bring up the rear, Sergeant, and . . ." Then he stop-

ped, for Sergeant Morris was slowly lower-
ing the limp body of Jimmy Leach to the
roadside.

"What about Leach, sir?" Morris asked,
and he was panting, though he had carried
his burden no more than a hundred yards.

Captain Johnson groaned inwardly. The
saving of an entire army was more important
than the life of a single private. Nevertheless
he hated having to do it, but he knew that
he had no choice. He was going to leave a
man behind.

"Carry him into the trees," he said curtly.
"Leave him a full water-bottle, some food,
some cigarettes and . . ."

"You're not going to leave him, sir, are
you?" Hooky Walker's tone betrayed his
utter disbelief. "You . . . you can't leave
Jimmy, alone!"

"Walker, there's a war on," Captain Johnson said stiffly. "I'm sorry about this, but
demolishing bridges is our job—and a vital
one. Carry him into . . ."

"I'll stay with him, sir," Hooky volun-
teered. "I mean . . . well, we've been pals
ever since . . ."

24

"There's nobody staying with him," Captain Johnson said. "In this situation every man is needed. Now, carry him into the trees. Better take one of his identity discs."

Hooky gaped. "Take one of his identity discs." Even Hooky could guess what that meant. Captain Johnson didn't give poor old Jimmy a dog's chance of getting home. If he did not die in the jungle through his wound, he would die by a Jap bullet or a bayonet.

Speechless, Hooky picked up his friend and carried him into a tiny clearing some twenty yards from the road. He laid him in as comfortable a position as he could, a full water-bottle by his side and put his own case containing just five cigarettes in Jimmy's pocket, then reluctantly took off one of the identity discs. From the disc, news could go back home that Private James Leach, R.E. was "Missing, presumed dead." Hooky choked over the thought.

Two minutes later he rejoined Captain Johnson on the road, and the march northwards began. Somewhere ahead was a tired army. Units would be regrouping to act as rearguards for the morrow. Others would snatch an hour's sleep, then trudge on. The blowing of the bridge had given the army a breathing space. Twenty miles on was the Chaukyi bridge. That, too, must be demolished. There was no time to worry over Jimmy Leach. He was a regrettable but unavoidable casualty of the war. Johnson sighed and tried to turn his thoughts to the job which lay ahead.

2. Behind the Jap lines

HOOKY PICKED UP the galvanometer and falling in behind Sergeant Morris took up his step with them automatically. As he went on, however, his lips were moving as he soundlessly counted every stride he took. When the count reached four hundred he broke the silence with a request:

"Can I fall out, Sarge? my boot-lace is undone."

"Don't dally. Better give the galvanometer to Harrison," Sergeant Morris said, and when the precious instrument had been handed over, the march went on, with Hooky bending over to retie a boot-lace which had never been undone.

Only when they had been marching again for several minutes did Sergeant Morris half turn to look back. He quite expected to see the tall, burly figure of Hooky Walker hurrying in the rear, faintly outlined by the moon, but the road was empty. He swore to himself then called to Captain Johnson:

"Sir, I think we've lost Walker. He stopped to tie his boot-lace."

"I know he did," Captain Johnson said irritably. "What's the fellow up to? Give him a shout and . . . no, no, don't shout. Hm!" He stood staring back along the moon-lit road, then rubbed his chin and the two days of stubble produced a slight rasping sound. "You don't think the Japs have got across already, Sergeant, do you? I suppose they could have picked him up."

"I shouldn't think so, sir," the sergeant mused, shaking his head. "He's not very bright, but nobody's going to sort of grab him without him making a fuss. They might shoot him from cover—but if they had done that we'd have heard the report, wouldn't we?"

"Well, if the Japs haven't jumped him, and he hasn't been shot, what the heck has happened to him? After all, he isn't going to wander off the road, is he? It isn't like walking through the jungle."

"I dunno, sir," Sergeant Morris said slowly; then as if he had suddenly made up his mind he said briskly, " I think he's just turned back."

"Turned back! What—Oh, for pete's sake, you don't mean he's gone back to Leach?"

"That's my guess sir. They were pals!"

Captain Johnson swore softly. It had been hard enough to leave Leach, but there had been no other way for him. As an Engineer he was needed, and dare not wait. He looked at his watch, and had to cup it in his hand to make the luminous dial show up. He was trying to make up his mind whether he dare risk going back. Sergeant Morris guessed what he was thinking and said:

" We wouldn't find him, sir. If he heard us coming he'd just slip off into the jungle and that'd be that. He's not particularly brilliant, but in this sort of country he's the cat's whiskers. If he's decided to stay with Leach . . . he will, and we won't find either of them."

"All right, quick march!" and they turned their faces northwards again, walking hard in an effort to catch up with the stragglers of the retreating army.

Hooky had waited only until the murmur of boots on the dusty road died away. Then he rose, and leaving the road for the ground where his boots would make even less sound, he trotted back the way he had come, counting again every stride until he had retraced the distance of four hundred paces.

He looked for some object which would tell him he was opposite the spot where he had left the road with Jimmy Leach in his arms. In the pale moonlight everything looked the same. The tops of the trees shut out the sky and the stars. Standing on the road was like being in a narrow valley, the tall trees like cliffs rising up on each side.

Hooky stood as still as a rock. He could hear voices quite near him. The river was not two hundred yards away, and already the Japanese engineers were hard at it, trying to construct a temporary bridge so that their infantrymen could carry on the running fight with the British and Indian army.

He walked into the fringe of the trees. Hooky opened his mouth once, meaning to call to Jimmy. He felt sure the youngster would have regained consciousness by now, and would answer his call. He decided not to shout. For all he knew Jap patrols might have swum across the river, and be establishing a bridge-head ready for the dawn. A shout would bring them, guns cocked, ready at the least sound to spray the jungle with lead.

For three hours Hooky Walker prowled about, going down on his hands and knees at the foot of scores of trees, feeling vainly for a body, but without success. Then, completely tired out, he sat down and leaning his back against a tree closed his eyes and dropped off to sleep. He could do that anywhere. Those who knew him swore that he had an alarm clock built in his brain, for he could also waken at any given time, and always to within a minute or so.

This night he did not set his mental

alarm clock, and when he did wake it was to freeze in sudden horror. He could hear voices; the high pitched voices of Japanese soldiers.

Day had come and the air was alive with insects. They flitted in and out of the narrow shafts of sunlight penetrating the treetops, and looked like spots of gold until they flew out of the sunshine again.

Stealthily Hooky felt for his tommy-gun, and sweat broke out on his forehead when his searching fingers failed to find it. Only when he hitched himself into a sitting position did he see the weapon. In the night he had slid down from a sitting to a lying position, and turning over had moved away from his gun.

Quietly he picked it up and cocked it. Then he sat listening. In his search during the night he had gone round and round, and had finally finished up within ten yards of the road. Through a thin screen of shrubs he could see men moving. An hour earlier the Japanese engineers had completed a makeshift bridge, capable of taking a single file of men, and the infantry were crossing,

32

Cautiously, he pushed his way through the trees . . .

forming up almost opposite where Hooky was sitting then moving off northwards.

"They're like a lot of flipping monkeys," he muttered, and grunted his disgust at the high pitched voices. Nevertheless, when he moved he did so with the utmost caution. Monkeys he might think the Japanese to be, but he knew they were fanatically brave. It was the kind of blind, obedient bravery which would send them walking over a cliff if they thought the Emperor demanded it.

Hooky wormed his way gradually away from the road, then began again to search for Leach. He had left his water-bottle with the unconscious Jimmy, and now he was thirsty; very thirsty. When he first woke dew had been dropping off the shiny leaves; but the sun had soon licked up all that. The ground was bone dry, and until he found Jimmy and the water-bottle the nearest liquid was the river.

"And a fat lot of chance I have of drinking out of that before night," he growled.

He searched an area which he was sure was the one where he had left his pal, but without seeing even the least sign which would tell him he was in the right spot. There was no sign of footmarks: just sun-dried leaves, oven-baked earth, ants by the million, and tormenting insects.

He patted the pockets of his bush-shirt, felt a faint something in one of them and grinned when his probing fingers brought out the stub of a cigarette. He looked towards the unseen road. At this distance he could hear only a vague murmur, punctuated now and then by a shout as some officer cursed and slapped a soldier who was slow at obeying a command.

Hooky struck a match on his thumb-nail and within seconds was enjoying his first smoke for over twelve hours. It was then that he heard a sound which made him nip the lighted end of his cigarette and put the stub behind his right ear so quickly that a glowing spot of tobacco burned the skin. He pressed a finger on the spot, then moved towards the sound. It was a cough—the kind of choking cough a man makes who is drinking water so thirstily that some has gone down the "wrong" throat.

He rounded the bole of a massive *sal* tree,

whose spreading branches towered ninety feet above the ground, and there was Jimmy, his back to another tree, and the water-bottle at his lips.

"Jimmy! I've been looking for . . ." and there Hooky's voice trailed off into silence. He had bounded into the open and was within a few yards of his friend when the man turned, the water-bottle was dropped, and an ugly-looking Jap pistol was thrust at Hooky's stomach.

The Britisher's one consolation in the first second or so was sight of his friend lying on the ground a yard or so further on. It was a momentary consolation, however, as he reminded himself that a Japanese soldier was pointing a gun at him.

"The water!" Hooky said, horror in his voice, and pointed down at the water-bottle. It had been dropped, and water was gurgling out of it into the dirt. Hooky's horror had been genuine enough, for his throat was now so dry that he was beginning to feel as if his tongue was swollen. Yet his cry did have an effect. The Japanese soldier looked down for an instant.

If Captain Johnson had been there then he would have realised what Sergeant Morris meant when he insisted that though Hooky was "not particularly brilliant—but in this country he is the cat's whiskers." As the man sitting there looked down for a split second, Hooky's foot came up. The revolver was kicked out of the soldier's hand, to go sailing a yard or so away. There followed a dull *thwack*, and a softer *bump*. The *thwack* was when Hooky's fist hit him full on the chin, the *bump* was when the back of the man's head struck the tree behind him.

Without bothering to see if the Jap was really "out," Hooky dropped a hand to the water-bottle and snatched it upright, so that the precious water ceased to run away. He wiped the lip of the bottle and allowed himself the luxury of a mouthful. He quickly rinsed his mouth, and was about to spit the water out when the lightness of the water-bottle warned him that there was little enough left.

"Well, they say you've got to eat a peck of dirt before you die," he murmured after swallowing the water. " Though I reckon there was more'n a spoonful of dust in that flippin' mouthful."

Recorking the bottle he stood it near Jimmy Leach, then after looking at the Japanese soldier for a moment, he strode across and picked up the revolver. It was a long-barrelled, ugly weapon, but it was fully loaded. Hooky pushed at the safety catch. Then, not sure whether it was in the " on " or " off " position, he took out one round of ammunition, centred the empty chamber over the firing position, and pulled the trigger. Now knowing which was the " off " position for the weapon, he carefully loaded the empty chamber again.

By this time the man he had knocked out was making vague attempts to heave himself into a sitting position. His eyes were glazed, and he began to speak in a slurred murmur.

To Hooky's astonishment the words were English. And when the man was shaking his head to clear the mists from his brain, and at the same time lifting shaky hands to feel the rising lump on the back of his head,

Hooky's fist hit the man full on the chin.

Hooky knelt before him and poking him in the ribs with the barrel of the revolver snapped:

"Now, name an' number, matey, or I'll blow you right across River Jordan . . . and them as crosses Jordan don't come back."

The flickering eyes steadied, the man shook his head again, then in a voice in which amazement, fear and joy were strangely mixed he said:

"Sahib, you are English. Tell me, you *are* English. I am *Jemadar* Bannerjee of the Burma Rifles. What you call Sergeant Bannerjee. I am Indian, from Rangoon. I became a soldier when *Japani* soldiers threaten invasion."

"Now look, *Jemadar* Banny-whatever-you-said, don't try that guff with me," Hooky said threateningly. "I might look simple, but I can tell a Jap rig-out and I know a Jap revolver when I hold one, see," and he poked the terrified man in the ribs again.

"Sahib, I can explain," and two shaking hands were held out appealingly to Hooky.

"I walk and fight from Rangoon, all the way up-country. Look at my feet . . . oh, I take off these shoes," and he dragged off a pair of the Japanese army rubber and canvas footwear, then held up one foot for Hooky to examine. "See . . . I am in pain all the time I walk. Blisters and blisters . . . so I am left behind."

"You managed to get here, didn't you!" Hooky was not convinced.

"Last night I am with Gloucester regiment . . . rearguard fighting," the man said, his eyes fixed on Hooky's grim face. "I cannot keep up. I have to hide in jungle. *Japani* soldiers pass me. They are everywhere. I think I shall be killed. You are listening, plees."

"I'm listening," Hooky agreed, his gaze straying occasionally to where Jimmy Leach was lying. He seemed to be moving a little. "Go on, and make it good. I'm not used to fairy tales."

"I tell only truth," the man protested. "Last night I begin to walk towards river. There are lights, so I am moving downstream a little and I meet *Japani* soldier.

41

He did not see me until it was too late. So, I take his uniform . . . see, sahib, my own uniform is beneath."

He tore open the Japanese shirt, to reveal a sweat-stained khaki bush-jacket. When he took off the Japanese shirt the regimental markings on the shoulder were those of the Burma Rifle Brigade.

He produced his army pay-book, and finally Hooky was convinced the man was telling the truth. Terrified at being left behind he had changed into Japanese uniform, and in the early hours of the morning, while the Japanese engineers were working like ants to construct a makeshift bridge, *Jemadar* (Sergeant) Bannerjee had gone downstream and managed to swim across the river.

Exhausted, he had slept for a few hours, only to be wakened by the sound of Japanese troops on the march. Crawling further into the jungle, he had come across Jimmy Leach, and had been enjoying a much needed drink when Hooky discovered him.

Satisfied the man was a genuine Indian, Hooky turned his attention to Jimmy Leach. They gave him half of the water left in the water-bottle, then looked at his wound. Here Bannerjee was able to help.

When Hooky brought out his own First Field Dressing Bannerjee felt in the Japanese tunic.

"Sahib, this is *Japani* soldier's First Aid pack. There is very good powder in it which stops infection in wounds caused by dirt."

"Oh, blimey, yes," Hooky had heard of the little capsule of *Teraboru* powder. Like the sulpha drugs used in the Western world to kill germs, the *Teraboru* powder if sprinkled on to an open wound, was a wonderful germicide. They sprinkled some on Jimmy's head wound, then bandaged it.

Leach could remember nothing of his bravery on the bridge, and reluctantly they gave him the last of their water. Then came the long wait for night. Bannerjee, whom Hooky decided to call Banji, thought they should cross the road when it was quiet and then strike up-country. He spoke Burmese fluently, and he thought if they could go from jungle village to jungle village, they might eventually get clear out of Burma and across into India itself.

43

"The idea's good," Hooky agreed, "but there are two things we need before we can move a yard. We need water and chow."

"Chow, sahib?" Bannerjee was puzzled by the word.

"Were you never eddicated?" Hooky asked. "Chow means grub, fodder, y'know," and he rubbed his stomach, at which Bannerjee's eyes opened wide and he laughed.

"That is word I must remember, sahib," he agreed. "Chow! Grub! Fodder! These are all new names to me for food. I am learning."

"Yeah, well if you listen to me you'll learn a lot," Hooky said, winking, "Now, as I was saying, we need water and we need food. So we can't move from here till we get some. To-night we'll go down to the river . . . fill the water-bottle, then see if there's any chance of getting some grub."

The corners of Bannerjee's mouth turned down at the idea of trying to get food from the Japanese; but he said nothing. Twice during the day the two crawled near enough to the north-south road to watch the traffic. Some wounded soldiers came walking past,

44

evidence that the British were still fighting a tough rearguard action.

Going northwards, however, with the temporary bridge already widened, were guns drawn by mules, endless columns of infantrymen, and mule-drawn supply carts laden with sacks of rice. The road was crowded from then until sunset, by which time Hooky had taken his belt in two holes, and was reduced to sucking a pebble to keep his mouth from drying up completely.

Bannerjee's feet were in bad shape, and though he was quite ready to accompany Hooky when darkness shrouded the jungle again, his offer was refused.

"I've been thinkin'," Hooky said. "Mebbe it will be better for only one of us to cross the river. We'll both go down for water, and you can take the water-bottle back so Jimmy can get rid of his thirst. While you are doing that I'll go across and see if I can scrounge anything."

"It will be very dangerous," Bannerjee protested. "Is it wise?"

"Look, my innards are crying out for food," Hooky said quietly. "I can manage without cigs. I can manage without beer, whisky, I can manage without going to the 'flicks,' but I gets downhearted when I'm hungry."

They went down to the river just as the moon was rising and came out on the bank about eighty yards downstream from the bridge. There were small lamps burning at each end of the bridge and they could see Japanese soldiers on sentry duty there.

"Wish I'd some flippin' guncotton to blow that bridge up," Hooky sighed as he stepped into the river and began scooping up water. He drank until he could drink no more. Then he watched Bannerjee go off with the water-bottle full to the cork.

"You will be very careful, sahib," the Indian pleaded. "What shall I do with the other sahib if you do not come back?"

"Don't start putting flowers on my grave yet," Hooky said solemnly. "I *am* coming back, and when I do I'll have the week's groceries with me."

"Groceries, sahib?"

"Grub, food . . . you're the dimmest bloke

*Standing in the river, he filled the water-
bottle.*

I've come across," Hooky said, "Go on, hop it, and don't spill any of that water."

When Bannerjee had gone, Hooky sat with his feet in the water and stared across the river. It presented a far different picture than it had on the previous night. While the Japanese had been waiting for the bridge to be made good again they had set up a staging post. Bamboo had been cut down, split, and woven into cooking shelters. Fed by dry bamboo the cooking fires burned well, and a continual stream of soldiers followed one another down to the cookhouse to have their tin food-bowls filled with a mixture of rice and meat—though the meat ration was small by European standards.

At length, as the queue began to shorten, Hooky partly waded, partly swam across the river. Huddled against the south bank he could smell the food being doled out, and it made his mouth water. He had been hungry before, but smelling hot food redoubled his hunger.

He waited until the queue of soldiers were served, and the cooks finally went off duty.

A stillness fell over the scene, and the only movement was the occasional walking across the bridge of one of the sentries to have a word with his fellow guard on the far side.

Hooky moved upstream, hugging the bank until he was opposite the cookhouses. There were three of them, and he could see the pinky glow of the cooking fires through the hastily plaited bamboo walls. There was no sign of life.

Hugging the ground, Hooky made his way up the bank, and lay at the side of the nearest shelter. Here he was completely hidden from the view of the bridge sentry. All he had to do was slip round the end of the bamboo wall into the cookhouse, get whatever he could, then slide back the way he had come without disturbing any of the sleeping troops.

"It ain't going to be easy taking a bowl of cooked rice an' chops across the river," he murmured, and grinned at the idea of such an undertaking. Chops! The very word made his mouth water. "If there are any chops they'll be big 'uns, for they'll be bullock chops, or better still water buffalo

49

chops. Strike a light, what a mouthful it'd be. Hm! Well, if you stay here much longer you won't even get a mouthful o' rice."

He rose and slipped quickly and quietly round the end of the shelter and into the three-sided cookhouse. He was conscious of three things immediately. The first was the delicious smell of cooking meat. The second was the tremendous heat from the cooking fires, on which stood three huge cauldrons, with their contents bubbling away. The third, and quite unexpected, was the sight of a man rising from a bench.

The figure was that of the night cook. He was there to make sure there was an adequate supply of cooked rice ready for the troops who would be moving on next morning, and to provide a meal for men arriving late from the south. He was stripped to the waist and had been lying down for a few minutes. One thing he had not expected was the sudden appearance of a white man.

For a second or so both men were so completely taken by surprise that they just gaped. Then Hooky made a grab. There were troops all around, and a yell of alarm would bring men by the score.

There should have been no struggle at all, for Hooky was almost twice the weight of his opponent, and certainly much stronger. Unfortunately for him the Jap was a skilled exponent of ju-jitsu. Hooky never really knew what happened to him.

One moment his powerful hands were within inches of clutching at the gaping Japanese cook, the next Hooky was turning a clumsy kind of cartwheel, while the cook was screaming for help, and beginning to run.

3. Bannerjee of the Burma Rifles

As HE FELL Hooky hit something hot. He could feel the furnace-like heat of the cooking fire, and to save himself from being burned, he turned and pushed himself away. In doing so, he accidentally upset one of the huge cauldrons of boiling rice. Flames, a yard high, were released, lighting up the cookhouse and the surrounding area.

Hooky was still too bemused by his sudden upset to know what had happened; but a second later he was electrified by a fiendish scream, a scream of mingled terror and pain. The Japanese cook had not been quite quick enough. He had been darting round the front of the simmering cauldrons when enough rice for several hundred men had poured out on to the ground in a spreading grey flood. His first scream had been of fear when he realised the cauldron was tipping over: his second one of pain as

the rice, like hot glue, covered his feet, up
to his ankles.

There came a questioning shout from the
guard at the bridge-head. He grabbed the
lamp and came running, staring in goggle-
eyed amazement at the antics of the cook
who was leaping about like a madman,
trying to shake scalding hot rice from his
feet.

The guard raced to first one cookhouse,
then the second, and finally to the third.
It was then that Hooky heaved the second of
the three big cauldrons over. The guard
saw him, dropped his lamp and was level-
ling his rifle for a shot when the flood of
rice from the second cauldron swept on to
him.

He was protected by puttees and the usual
baggy trousers of a Japanese infantryman,
but the flood of hot rice sent him off balance
and his shot went through the roof of the
cookhouse.

By this time men were stirring in the
nearby trees, grabbing for their weapons,
half-afraid that the rearguard of the British

army had come back and was making a surprise night raid.

The guard from the north side of the river had come running, and though he was unable to understand why the cook and the first guard were hopping about like crazy puppets, he did not make the mistake of his comrade in rushing to the cookhouse. He fired a shot through the plaited bamboo wall, and bellowed a challenge.

The bullet ripped through the bamboo, making Hooky jump. He could see the figures of men beginning to take shape in the darkness of the trees, their forms just visible in the red light from the two un-covered kitchen fires. For the moment the flames saved the Britisher, for they effectively masked him from the outside. One thing was certain, they could not mask him for long, for the heat was unbearable. He tried to smash through the back of the hut, but the bamboo was too tough. It was new, and heavy, and would have resisted an axe for many minutes before giving.

Hooky had the revolver he had taken from *Jemadar* Bannerjee, and he drew it

The boiling grey flood swept over his feet.

from the holster now, flicked the safety to the " off " position, and crouching behind the one cauldron still thrumming away on its fire, waited. He was cursing his own stupidity in not making sure the Japanese had left their cookhouse unguarded.

" You don't think, Hooky," he muttered. " That's your flippin' trouble. Bull-headed, you are. Now you've had your chips. Cor, look at 'em. Hundreds of 'em."

Hooky was right. There were hundreds of Japanese soldiers milling about uneasily in the shelter of the trees. No one quite knew what was happening. They had heard screams, a shot, and even now the cook was groaning and whimpering. The guard whose puttee-protected legs had been washed in scalding rice, was scraping the stuff off with the back of his bayonet, and thanking his stars that he had not been bare-legged.

Then an officer appeared. He slapped the face of the guard, demanding to know what had happened. The second guard, also had his face slapped when he could offer no explanation of the screams.

" I saw nothing," the first guard said,

wiping his rice-covered bayonet on the seat of his baggy trousers. "I heard a scream. I saw the cook jumping about like a madman. Then I came running. As I reached the cookhouse one of the big cauldrons toppled over, and I was lucky not to be scalded as the cook was."

"Get in the cookhouse and see what is wrong!" the officer snapped, "And fetch the idiot cook here. Raising the alarm as if the enemy were back. Probably only a support gave way. Nobody saw anyone, did they?" and he looked round.

Bullet-shaven heads were shaken. The soldiers beginning to draw closer had certainly seen nothing. They had wakened to screams and a shot. Three of them, with bayonets fixed on the ends of their long rifles, began to advance towards the cookhouse. They were small men, and two of them wore glasses. In the dancing red light of the cookhouse fires their rifles looked much too large for them, but Hooky had no false ideas about Japanese infantry. They might be small, they might be cruel, but they were good soldiers. Unless they were shot dead they would come into the cookhouse, and they were no novices with the bayonet.

The chattering among the other soldiers scattered among the trees died down. Some of them dropped to one knee, and for a few seconds the only sounds were those made by the fires, the cauldron of rice, and the river as it rippled along some ten feet behind and below the cooking shacks.

Rifles in the " on guard " position, the three soldiers got to within six paces of the cookhouse. Hooky, peering cautiously round the one remaining cauldron was already taking aim when the silence was broken:

" Tac-a-taca-taca-taca-taca-taca !"

From the bridge-head some fifty yards away spots of fire began to wink in the night, and the silence gave place to the frightening chatter of a machine-gun. Two of the three soldiers went down, their rifles clattering to the ground. The third swung round and fired a shot towards the bridge, then sagged backwards like a tired doll.

The officer and the N.C.O.'s clustered near him dived for cover as the machine-gun fired another burst. It stopped, and then, beginning with one rifle, a ragged fusillade began as soldiers took aim for the spot from which the winking pin-points of fire had come.

Hooky Walker could scarcely believe it. He had been ready to drop the three Japanese in their tracks, then try and make a run for the river.

"Strike a light," he murmured. "Cor, luv a duck," and with that he nipped smartly out of the cookhouse, turned right along its side, and slithered down the bank in a cloud of dust.

No one heard the splash as he went into the river. Rifles were cracking everywhere, every man firing at the bridge-head from which there was now no sound at all. Then, with a thunderous roaring of its motor, a small car was driven into position and its headlights switched on.

The crackle of rifles died away at once, for there was no one at the bridge-head. A superstitious shudder went through many of the nearest soldiers. They had seen the winking spurts of flame from the machine-gun. It had come from the bridge-head. Now there was no sign of gunner or gun.

"Taca-taca-tac-taca-tac!" The machine-gun came to life again with a short, vicious burst, and one of the car headlamps went out. The firing this time had come from halfway across the bridge, and a hundred rifles were lifted again, and a crashing volley of shots shattered the night silence once more.

The driver of the small car had escaped injury when his headlamp was shattered and with commendable bravery he swung his vehicle round until the single beam of his other headlight shone across the middle of the bridge. It lit up a machine-gun, but there was no man with it.

Those who had shivered before, shivered again. What was this? Was there a ghost behind the gun? Men drew back, suddenly afraid they might be called upon to go over the bridge and attempt to capture gun and ghostly gunner.

In the river, Hooky was swimming the deeper part of the channel, and making heavy weather of it. He was a powerful swimmer, but despite the danger, he had filled the pockets of his tunic with some tins he had seen in the Japanese cookhouse. They had bumped heavily against his thighs when he made his dash for the river bank. Now they dragged at him like some Old Man of the Sea, and by the time he could feel bottom once more he was almost too exhausted to walk.

He heard the machine-gun burst from the middle of the bridge. He saw the car headlight illuminate the weapon, and he, too, gaped, when he realised there was no one with the gun.

Then, with the light from the cookhouse fires throwing a faint pink glow more than half-way across the river, Hooky plodded wearily through the shallowing waters to the bank. He stumbled along for a few yards after laboriously climbing the bank, then catching one foot in a tree root, plunged face down.

He lay spreadeagled, meaning to rest for a minute or so, then go on to rejoin *Jemadar* Bannerjee and Jimmy Leach. Instead his eyes closed. Hard marching from the days when the retreat northwards began, little rest, and not enough food were a combination which had sapped even his great strength, and sleep overwhelmed him.

He came back to consciousness with his heart thumping wildly and gooseflesh creeping up his temples. The short hairs on the back of his neck were tingling. Even before he opened his eyes he knew something had happened.

Making no attempt either to open his eyes or move he listened. Jungle cocks were crowing and their challenging, shrill *cock-a-doodle* told him where he was. There was no mistaking the crowing of a jungle cock. Whereas the farmyard cock crows *cock-a-doodle-dooo*! the jungle variety leaves off the last *dooo*.

It was dawn, though the sun would not be up. The jungle cocks were early risers! Hooky could drop off to sleep in much the same way that a light goes out when the switch is flicked up. He woke in the same way. One moment fast asleep, the next wide awake.

He was conscious now that something hard was pressing against his forehead, and he knew without looking that it was the muzzle of a gun, probably the muzzle of a revolver! With an effort he drew in a great breath and pretended to sigh as if about to wake. The gun muzzle pressed a little harder against his forehead, then a voice he knew said:

"No need to pretend, sahib. You are wide awake. Turn over, open your eyes, and do not make a sound."

Hooky obeyed. His muscles were taut as a drawn bowstring. Given a split second chance he would make a grab for the gun; but there was no chance. *Jemadar* Bannerjee had eased himself out of range. To Hooky's surprise the Indian then flipped the heavy Jap revolver round and leaning forward held it out butt first.

"I am sorry if I startle you, sahib," he said, smiling apologetically, "but very necessary you wake quietly. *Japani* soldiers coming soon. Must make no sound, or be caught."

"The Japs . . ." the news caught Hooky

so off-guard that for a moment he hardly realised that the man he had looked on a moment earlier as a foe had given him the revolver. "Where? And . . . here, what the flippin' heck is going on? You waken me with a gun muzzle driving a hole through my forehead, then you hand it over. What are you? Where are . . ."

"Sahib, must be quiet," Bannerjee pleaded. "I put gun against head so you will make no sound. Sorry for that. But I speak truth when I say *Japani* soldiers already across bridge, and coming into jungle . . . here. Maybe looking for us."

"For us!" and suddenly even more startled Hooky sat up and asked. "What about Jimmy? Where is . . ."

"Here," and Bannerjee pointed to a bush about six yards away. "I carry . . ."

Hooky did not stay to hear more. He rushed across to the bush, drew a branch aside and there was young Leach. His eyes were open, but he made no move until Hooky spoke to him. Then, cautiously, he turned his head and a weak smile crossed his face.

"Hooky!—— What's been happening?"

"It is you, Hooky?" he asked. "Or am I imagining things again. I was picked up a few minutes ago by a bloke . . . I thought he was a Jap, except that he handled me gently."

"Are you okay, Jimmy?" and anyone who had dealt with Hooky Walker at normal times would have been amazed at the gentleness in the big fellow's voice.

"Okay? Be your age, Hooky. Apart from the fact that I feel as if a water buffalo had dug its horns into the back of my head, and my innards feel as if they've forgotten what food is like, I'm fine. I'll bet if I tried hard my legs might hold me up. What's been happening? Where are we? And why do I feel as if I'd been under a steam roller or something."

Jimmy could remember nothing about the incident when he dragged the C.O. of the Gloucesters off the bridge, seconds before it was destroyed. He was introduced to the smiling Bannerjee.

"I came back with the water-bottle, sahib," he told Hooky, "gave Jimmee a drink as you ordered. Then waited for you

66

to return—maybe with some food. I wait and wait and wait. Nothing happens. Then I creep down to riverside, near bridge. I see light from *Japani* cooking shelters, and I wonder what is happening to you. Later I hear a scream."

"Yeah, that was when I upset the first great big boiler of rice," Hooky chuckled. "I thought I was done for. I grabbed a little Jap cook, and before you could count one he'd thrown me over like I was a half-pound string o' sausages. And you heard him, Banji?"

"Yes. Then I see guard on other side of river run, and I hear rifle shot. Guard on my side of river then run across bridge. I am afraid for you, sahib . . . so I crossed bridge also."

"You did?" Hooky stared open-mouthed before giving a low whistle and saying: "Cor, that was taking a risk, wasn't it? What if they'd caught you?"

"I am frightened for your sake," Banner-jee confessed. "On far side of bridge I see soldiers waking up, and guard going towards end cookhouse. Then three soldiers come and also move towards end cookhouse. Then I guess you are there."

"You never said a truer word," Hooky admitted. "I was there, like a flippin' rat in a trap. I reckoned I was going to lose my ticket, an' no mistake. Then somebody started blasting off with a machine-gun. Strike a light, I could have wept on his flippin' shoulder with relief. I don't know who it was, but . . ."

"It was me, *Jemadar* Bannerjee, sahib," the Indian said proudly. "There was a machine-gun post set up at bridge head. I swung machine-gun round and fired a burst. Then I pick up gun and run for middle of bridge. I think maybe *Japani* soldiers fire at me."

"They did, too," Hooky agreed. "There must have been a hundred of them rattling off. Good thing you moved. And did you fire from the middle of the bridge?"

"Yes, sahib. I shoot out one light of motor car, then I run for it."

"Sounds as if you've both been busy," Jimmy said, feeling gingerly at the bandaged part of his skull.

"You could call it that, if you like," Hooky said solemnly, and began to fumble with the tiny cluster of oak leaves pinned to his tunic over the pocket. When he had unfastened the pin he turned to Bannerjee and asked:

"Know what this is?"

"No, sahib?"

"It's a kind of medal. You get it for being mentioned in despatches," Hooky explained. "I got this for a little job I did on the beaches at Dunkirk. There happened to be a brass hat watching when I did it. There were no brass hats, unless they were Jap brass hats, watching you last night; but I reckon your action rated a mention in despatches, just the same. Sit still, or else I'll be pricking my flipping finger, and I don't want to get blood poisoning just now." And with that he pinned the little cluster of bronze oak leaves on Bannerjee's chest. Then he solemnly shook hands with the equally solemn-faced Indian.

"Shake hands with him, Jimmy," he ordered. "If I was a cat with nine lives, last night wouldn't have mattered; but since I've only got one life, he helped me keep my skin whole. And if I'd copped out, you wouldn't be on your way to India at this minute would you?"

"Am I on my way to India?" Jimmy asked, straightening up so that he could offer his right hand to Bannerjee. "I've got the feeling that I'm sitting under some bug-ridden bushes, and I'm that hungry I could eat the hind leg of an elephant, *and* its toe-nails."

That reminded Hooky of something, and from the capacious pockets of his bush-jacket he produced six tins of Japanese emergency rations. Since none of them could read Japanese they had no idea what the tins contained until they opened one. Hooky sniffed at the contents and pulled a wry face.

"Fish," he said. He attempted to get some of the *bonito* out of the tin, and found it was compressed so hard as to be almost solid. With a grunt of disgust he said: "Well, I reckon a bit of this should go a long way, eh Banji. We'll open one tin at a time. I wonder if we are supposed to soak it. Some things you soak, and then they grow to about ten times the dry size."

"No time to soak, sahib," Bannerjee said soberly. "You hear what I hear? Axes." The Indian's hearing must have been very acute, for both Hooky and Leach had to listen intently before they heard the soft tck-tck-tck-tck of axes biting into palm treetrunks.

Digging some of the *bonito* from the tin, Hooky popped it into his mouth then handed knife and tin to Bannerjee, telling him to feed Jimmy, then eat the rest. He was going to investigate.

He crept through the jungle as noiselessly as a hunting cat. Ten minutes later he came back, and arrived so quietly that he startled both Leach and Bannerjee. The latter swallowed a piece of fish so hurriedly that he had a fit of coughing.

"Sorry, very sorry," Bannerjee spluttered, his eyes watering. "I not hear you come. I think I am nervous of *Japani* soldiers finding us."

"You needn't do any more worrying about that," Hooky said grimly. "Because they are going to find us. They're cutting down all the timber in this area. Some are using bicycle-chain saws, others axes. If they knew we were here they couldn't have cut off our retreat any surer. There must be a couple of hundred of the devils . . . there you are," and he shrugged as three trees crashed down within as many seconds. "They're in a semi-circle, and I reckon they've decided to clear the ground so no one can approach the bridge again without being seen."

Hooky's guess was right. The Japanese commander had decided that the ground on both sides of the northern approach to the bridge should be cleared of all but the big trees.

Throughout the morning the simple but highly efficient bicycle-chain saws ripped through the fairly soft trunks of palm trees while axes slashed down the thickets of bamboo.

There was no hope of escape for the two Britishers and Bannerjee the Indian. If they crept down to the river they would certainly be seen from the opposite bank. Nor could they steal through the semi-circle of sweating soldiers hacking away at the palm trees and undergrowth. The ring was too tightly closed for even a cat to have got through without being seen.

Towards noon, when the barrier between them and the Japanese had been reduced to less than thirty yards, Hooky turned to Jimmy Leach to ask:

"Can you swim?" and when Leach nodded Hooky went on: "Could you keep afloat for a mile?"

"You're not thinking of trying to get away downstream, surely?" Jimmy asked. "You said yourself there were Japs by the hundred milling about on the other bank. They'd riddle us with bullets before we'd gone a dozen yards."

"It's that or be bayoneted here," Hooky said grimly. "I've just had another peep at these woodmen, and they've got sentries every dozen yards. They're making sure that if there is anybody in here they don't get away."

Leach glanced at Bannerjee. The Indian looked grave, but made no comment.

"Have we a chance?" he asked helplessly.

"I dunno," Hooky was bluntly honest. "We've got a Jap revolver. I have a grenade left. I reckon there's at least a hundred men between us and freedom . . . so we can't fight our way out. Are you game to try the river?"

Leach nodded.

"Okay. Then stay here and wait for me. If you hear a row, or shots, you'll know I've bought it. You'll have to manage without pappa then," and he winked, then rose. "See you in a few minutes, lads. Don't get into mischief while I'm away." Then he slid off into the bush, heading for the sweating Japanese who were working as if their lives depended on clearing the ground completely before sundown.

"He is very brave man, Leach Sahib," Bannerjee said softly. "Very brave."

"Yes!" Somehow Jimmy Leach managed to jerk the one word out. There was a lump in his throat. Big Hooky Walker had befriended him ever since they first came out East. Now, unless a miracle happened, he was unlikely to see the big Yorkshireman again. Indian and Britisher sat and listened, waiting for the shot, or a commotion which would tell them that Hooky had been seen.

Suddenly the sound they had been dreading to hear broke the stillness. It was the brittle crump of a hand grenade, followed within seconds by the cracking reports of a revolver. There was a chorus of yells, then the sound of men running through the jungle. This was followed by the shrill screaming commands of an officer.

4. Hooky's 'flotilla'

JIMMY LEACH had scrambled to his feet at the growing pandemonium. He was quite pale despite his tan. Turning to Bannerjee who had also got to his feet he asked:

"Have you got a revolver . . . or a grenade?" Then as the Indian sadly shook his head Leach groaned, and muttered. "Why'd we let him go? We should have all gone together. If we . . ."

Crack—— crack! Two more revolver shots, and then a perfect fusillade of rifle shots. When the shooting stopped men were still yelling excitedly, but there was a new sound; the crackle of burning brushwood. This was a sound to be dreaded at this time of the year, for it was almost the end of the dry season in Burma, and the under-growth was tinder dry. A match could start a conflagration, which for Jimmy and Bannerjee could mean a ghastly death. They would be burned out of their hiding place. The shouting increased as the crackling grew louder. If the fire had begun in a bamboo thicket the tall yellow stems would burn like oil-soaked rags, for they are highly inflammable.

The first whorls of smoke began to drift down towards Jimmy and Bannerjee. Very quickly it thickened, until the light breeze which they had scarcely noticed before was bringing the acrid smell of burning bamboo and rotting undergrowth to bite at the nostrils and the back of the throat.

From the sound of the yelling it seemed as if half the Japanese army must be on the other side of the fire, and occasionally they could hear the shrill voice of an officer screaming commands.

Suddenly Hooky Walker appeared. His chest was heaving as if he had run a long, hard race, and there was a smear of blood on one cheek. He quietly wiped it away with the back of one hand.

"Was it a bullet?" Jimmy asked, moving towards him.

"Was what a bullet?" Hooky asked handing first Bannerjee then Jimmy, lengths of bamboo about an inch thick.

"Your cheek. Your cheek's all bloody."

"A scratch from a piece of bamboo," Hooky said, and reaching for the water-bottle gulped down a mouthful before saying: "Now, look, when the smoke thickens we get our chance. It'll be a slim one, but it is a chance. Come on . . . but don't be seen," and he led them towards the river bank.

They halted in a thin screen of bushes. Staring across the sunlit river they could see soldiers being hurriedly assembled, then marched across the rickety bridge. The Japanese C.O. did not want a big fire to start. Timber so near a road might be very useful later on, and if this fire got out of hand someone would slap him across the face for not taking care. He was organising fire-fighting squads as quickly as he could.

One and all, from the Jap C.O. down to the humblest private, were convinced that somewhere on the opposite bank of the river were the men who had staged the raid on the cookhouse the night before. Since he was sure the men were trapped in the patch of jungle between the fire and the river bank, the C.O. ordered a dozen riflemen to take up their position on the bank, ready to shoot anyone who showed on the far side. His own men were ordered not to approach the far bank of the river.

All were convinced that the rapidly growing fire would soon drive the Britishers out of their cover. The shooting and the shouting around the edge of the fire had died down. Men were flailing at the flames in an effort to bring them under control, while riflemen stood by to protect them.

"You mean we're going to try to get into the river?" Leach asked, and his mouth was dry at the very thought of it. "What about the Japs on the other bank? They're just waiting for us. We'll be like pepper-pots by the time they finish."

"How deep is the water, sahib?" Bannerjee asked, trying to keep his voice steady. "Will we be covered at once?"

"No! You've about a dozen yards to cover before the river deepens," Hooky admitted. "We've got to get through the shallows and under water before they open fire."

"Then stay under and drown, or pop up and be shot to rags," Jimmy Leach said grimly. "Okay, Hooky, I know you're not daft. Where's the trick?"

"This," and Hooky tapped the foot-long piece of bamboo he had kept for himself. "You sit on the river bed, stick one end of the bamboo just above the water and suck air through the other end."

Bannerjee and Leach exchanged quick glances, and neither looked very happy. It was left to Jimmy Leach to point out one thing Hooky had overlooked.

"But there'll be water in the tubes," he said tartly. "Once you get under you can't suck water out of the tube. If you do you'll have to swallow it, for the moment you uncover the end of the tube again it'll fill once more."

For a moment or so the burly Yorkshire-man was silent. Then he shrugged and admitted:

"I hadn't thought about that. It seemed a good idea. I knew there must be a snag, it was so simple. Well, it looks as if—here, half a tick. We could block the ends of the bamboo up, couldn't we? Then open 'em up again once we were in deep water."

It was the answer to the problem, and while the fire drew nearer and the smoke thickened until all three were coughing, they tore off their bush-jacket patch pockets and forced the cotton material into the open ends of the bamboo pipes.

"Now, when we get in deep water," Hooky cautioned, "keep together. We walk up, not downstream. The Nips will expect us to go downstream, and if there's any shootin'—it'll be downstream."

"And another thing," now it was Jimmy Leach with a piece of useful advice. "Grab a stone ... the heavier the better. You won't find it easy to stay under water, I can tell you that."

"Grab those tins of fish," Hooky said, picking one up for himself. "We'll need to eat later on, and in any case this stuff will help us keep on the river bed. The bit I ate feels like lead in my innards. Are you ready?"

They crept close to the bank. Clouds of smoke were drifting past them, going downstream like early morning mist on the river. The trouble was that it kept thinning as the breeze blew it along.

There were men on the far bank, watching intently. Nor did it help Hooky, Jimmy or Bannerjee when they realised that in addition to a score of men with rifles, there were three machine-guns posted. The Japanese were taking no chances of anyone getting away.

"When I say 'Go,' we run," Hooky said, screwing up his smarting eyes against the smoke. He watched for perhaps half a minute, then as another patch of bamboo caught fire, and the undergrowth threw off smoke, he yelled "Go!" and began to run.

They reached the river bank, slid down it at breakneck speed, and began to splash through the shallows to mid-channel where the river was much deeper and the current quite strong.

The officer standing behind the machine-gunners on the opposite bank screamed out a command as the three figures appeared, seen vaguely through the smoke screen. "Fire, fire, fire!"

Trigger fingers tightened and the *Nambu* light machine-guns stammered a chorus of death. The aim was too high, but it took no more than a second to depress the muzzles, and a sudden spattering of foam showed in the shallow waters. At the same instant all three figures flopped forward, and vanished.

The firing stopped, but the officer ordered them to fire again.

" Into the water . . . into the water," he screeched . . . " and lower down. They'll float with the current. They may only be wounded." Then to the infantrymen standing by he screamed : " Get downstream . . . and wade in. I want the bodies. I want to know if these men are just stragglers, or whether they are part of a force left to work behind our lines. Go on !" and he slapped the face of the nearest man.

" Tac-taca-taca-taca-taca-taca !" Hundreds of the .256 bullets kicked up little jets of water as they sprayed the centre of the river, until it looked as if a heavy tropical shower was beating down in midstream.

Below the surface a desperate battle for

life was going on. Hooky, Jimmy and Bannerjee escaped the second burst of machinegun fire by a split second, and though they could hear nothing but the roar of water in their ears as they plunged to the bottom, they knew what was going on.

From every bullet which smacked into the river came a shock wave. Hundreds of shock waves spread outward, and the three refugees, holding their breath and fighting to get their breathing tubes unblocked, felt the kick of each and every shock wave. It was as if unseen hands were pummelling them.

Jimmy let his bamboo slip from his fingers, and only caught it by a lucky upward thrust with his left hand.

Each man was at the end of his endurance by the time he had popped one end of the bamboo breathing-pipe into his mouth, pushed it upwards until the other end was above water, and whipped out the rag which blocked it. Luckily, the blistering hail of bullets whipping into the water had kept their hands hidden from the men ashore.

By the time this complicated procedure had been completed each of the trio had been forced to swallow a pint of river water.

They could breathe now. But it was not easy. It meant holding the tube with one hand while with the other they held on to the river bed. Fortunately the river bed was strewn with rocks of all shapes and sizes. Had it been sandy, the battle would have been lost in the first few minutes, for they would have quickly floated to the surface.

At the end of five minutes, when he was beginning to master the art of inhaling and exhaling through the bamboo pipe, Hooky cautiously picked his way across the river bed to the nearest figure. The river water was far from being crystal clear, and not until he was within a yard of him did he recognise Jimmy. Hooking one foot under a boulder to keep from being floated downstream by the current, he touched Jimmy Leach on the shoulder, and made a jabbing motion upstream.

Jimmy passed the signal on to Bannerjee, and then began the queerest journey any man ever made. They had to keep their bamboo breathing-tubes just above water. —not too high, in case anyone was still watching the river from the bank—they had to cling to whatever was handy to hold themselves on to the river bed. It took time. It was also exhausting. They had to remember to breathe only through the bamboo pipe, and every now and then would suck water in through their nostrils.

Bannerjee was the first to crack. Suddenly he rose, his legs wide to keep his balance, his head and shoulders above the surface. Hooky grabbed him, and pulled him under again, but he was too late. The Indian had dropped his bamboo, and could no longer breathe under water.

Splashing and struggling he broke free and began to stride uncertainly towards the bank. Hooky followed him, throwing away his own bamboo, and Jimmy Leach followed suit. They expected to hear shouts, perhaps shots, but nothing happened. Only when they got to the bank and dropped exhausted on the mud there did they realise

Underwater, Hooky breathed through his bamboo pipe.

that they had come further upstream than had seemed possible.

The shaky bridge was round a slight bend in the river. Hooky turned to Bannerjee who was face down, coughing up river water, and trying to apologise at the same time for his weakness.

"Not to worry, Banji. We were all tuckered out, anyway," Hooky said kindly. "Rest . . . we'll all rest. We've had it for now, anyway. I couldn't walk another yard if there was the biggest feed on earth only a stride away."

He turned and flopped face down on the mud. Jimmy Leach had already done that, and with the hot sun warming them they rested, and within minutes were asleep. The underwater ordeal had sapped what little strength they had had left.

From a clump of bushes a dozen yards upstream a man watched them. Then, when he was satisfied they really were asleep, he moved backwards without a sound and vanished. Above the tall trees a golden oriole was making the air ring with its calls. The river sang softly, and as a background to it all there was the buzz-buzz of jungle insects, large and small.

The sounds did not disturb the three sleepers. For weeks they had been playing a desperate game. Theirs had been the task of blowing up the bridges the moment the last of the weary troops passed over, then racing ahead to prepare to demolish the next bridge. Food had been short, sleep they had snatched in odd hours wherever they could. They had been very near the limit when they blew the last bridge. Now, having gone for a day and a half with only one tin of Japanese emergency rations between three of them, they had to rest. Their sleep was deep and long.

The sun dropped below the treetops. The harsh light of day softened. The sky turned pink, then blood red, then purple, and finally the stars came out, and still the trio slept.

They were still sleeping when through the jungle, soft-footed as a hunting tiger, someone approached. Whoever he was carried a small lamp, shaded so that it threw no more than a small circle of yellow light about itself.

The unknown came to the water's edge some thirty yards upstream from the three sleepers. For perhaps two minutes the tiny circle of light from the lamp remained still, then it began to move slowly downstream. Without a sound the bearer of the lamp drew nearer.

He laid something on the ground within a yard of Bannerjee's feet, stood for a moment or so as if adjusting the thing he had been carrying, then moved back. He picked up his lamp, and within a minute the night was as dark as it had ever been.

Sergeant Morris had said Hooky Walker was the " cat's whiskers " when it came to work in the jungle, and within minutes of the light disappearing he was proved right. Hooky stirred. He could not have heard anything, for the unknown had made no sound, yet some unconscious "sentry" in Hooky's mind warned him that something had happened.

He sat up. He wanted to yawn, but he stifled the desire and looked round. The river rippled softly in the darkness, and the sky above the river, seen through the tall trees, was beginning to pale a little as the moon rose. Its light dimmed the stars. When it rose higher it would shine down on the water and turn it to silver.

Hooky sniffed suspiciously, then whispered:

"You're asleep, Hooky my lad." But he sniffed again and murmured. "Well, if it is a dream it smells wonderful."

Cautiously he rose, taking care not to touch either Jimmy Leach or the snoring Bannerjee. He kept sniffing like a dog which smells a toothsome bone, and a few moments later his outstretched right hand touched something warm—warm, wet, and soft. Hooky explored with his hand.

"Cor, strike a light," he murmured. "It *must* be a flippin' dream. It can't be true." He dipped a thumb and forefinger into the warm stuff. It felt like cooked rice. He lifted a few grains to his mouth and cautiously tasted it. At once the salivary glands in his mouth came to life, and he knew that he was not dreaming. This thing he could not see—though his probing fingers had decided it felt like a bowl—contained cooked rice, and something more than cooked rice. The taste was of chicken.

"Wakey-wakey," Hooky whispered, gently shaking Jimmy Leach with one hand, Bannerjee with the other. "The flippin' dinner gong has gone. What'd you like first . . . rice with chicken, or would you like chicken followed by rice?"

Britisher and Indian woke at the first touch. Though they had been sound asleep, their bodies soaked with tiredness, their minds had not been at rest. They were wide awake at once.

"What did you say about chicken and rice?" Jimmy Leach asked, a hint of apprehension in his voice. "Have you gone barmy?"

"Smell this!" Hooky lifted the brass bowl and brought it round with a sweep of the arm so that it passed within a few inches of Jimmy and Bannerjee.

"Where's it come from?" Jimmy asked.

"Perhaps it is poisoned," Bannerjee said, though his mouth was watering at the smell.

"I don't know where it came from, Banji," Hooky said, putting the bowl down between the three of them. "But if you don't want to risk it, I'll eat your share and die with my tummy full. Whoever brought this needn't have bothered to cart poisoned food here. He could have finished us off with a jungle knife as easy as kiss your hand. Now, do you want to wait till the moon comes up, so nobody gets more than his share, or do you want to start eating now?"

They ate there and then. The brass bowl must have held almost a gallon of rice, and in the rice were three small jungle fowl, cooked to perfection. Starved though they were, even Hooky was satisfied by the time he was scraping the last few grains of rice from the side of the bowl.

"A cigar, a pint of beer, and I wouldn't change places with the Emperor of Japan," he said. Then: "Come to think of it, I wouldn't change places with the Emperor of Japan anyway. He doesn't know what's coming to him. Cor, I feel marvellous."

By this time the moon had risen above

the treetops, and they eased themselves into the shadow of a clump of bushes. The river was like a sheet of silver, and if a boat came down, quiet as the flowing waters itself, they would be seen sitting on the bank.

For almost an hour they discussed who their unknown benefactor could be. They were sure he, or she, must be a Burmese— perhaps from a nearby village. Why their unknown friend had not wakened them they could not guess, and finally they went to sleep again.

Just before dawn, when the jungle cocks were shattering the stillness with their shrill cries of *Cock-a-doodle* they had another visitor. Down the river bank came a small boy. He was bare to the waist, but wore a brilliantly coloured *lungyi*, the skirt-like garment which men and women wear in Burma. On his head was a brass bowl, and when he saw the three dirty soldiers were awake he halted. For a moment it seemed as if he would turn and fly. Then Bannerjee spoke to him. In that moment his knowledge of the Burmese tongue was priceless.

" You have nothing to fear," he called out.

"The blessings of Buddha be on you for the gift of food last night."

The youngster, a boy of about seven, smiled a little hesitantly then came forward and laid the second bowl on the ground. Like the first it contained a mound of snowy-white rice and cooked chickens. From his hips, tucked into the folds of the *lungyi* the boy brought out three chipped enamel mugs.

"The headman of our village sends you food," he said, and it was obvious he was reciting something which had been drummed into him by repetition. "We are friends of the British. We hate the Japanese. The headman asks you to stay here, where you will be safe, until he can arrange for one of the young men to guide you to safety." He cupped his hands together in a little gesture of obeisance, then stooping quickly, he picked up the empty bowl and was gone with a patter of feet.

"I've got friends all over the world," Hooky chuckled. "What did I tell you yesterday?"

"What did you tell us?" Jimmy asked,

taking one of the cups and dipping it into the rice with a scooping motion which collected a leg of chicken.

By the time they had emptied the bowl they were feeling on top of the world. They risked moving to the river, one at a time, to wash some of the accumulated dirt off. Hooky rubbed his big chin, his fingers producing a rasping noise which suggested a razor was long overdue.

" If I walked into a Jap now he'd die of fright at sight of me. Bet I look awful, eh, Jimmy."

Jimmy Leach was feeling better, and with a mock frown he drew back a pace as if to get a better view of his friend. Then he said solemnly:

" I'd say you are looking just how the best people should look. You've got that well groomed air about you. Sophisticated, y'know. Your clothes obviously come from Saville Row. As for your boots . . ."

" He jokes, yes?" Bannerjee asked, slightly puzzled.

" He'd better be," Hooky said, grinning. " If I thought he was taking the micky out

"The headman of our village sends you food . . ."

of me I'd take him in one hand and squeeze him till the juice ran out of him. Anyway, I feel good this morning. All we need is the flippin' morning paper, then we could read how the war was going on. As it is I think mebbe I'll just have a nap. Bring the coffee and cigars about eleven, Jimmy."

Even joking thoughts of coffee and cigars were forgotten two hours later, for the buzzing of insects was suddenly interrupted by the call of a tuk-tu lizard. Hooky and Jimmy had heard the call: "Tuk-too . . . tuk-too . . . t u k - t o o o" often enough during their time in Burma, and thought nothing of it. Bannerjee, however, was suddenly frightened. He knew the tuk-tu lizard was a night creature. It haunted the walls of houses, hunting mosquitoes. It rarely called by daylight.

The call came again, and Bannerjee whispered:

"Someone is near, sahib. Someone is signalling . . . I think maybe we are going to be captured."

He was wrong, for after giving the tuk-tu

lizard's call again, a man stepped into view. How he had got so close without being heard mystified the two Britishers, especially as he was an old man. He had a few white hairs on his chin and his face was wrinkled, giving him the appearance of a man between eighty and ninety years old. He wore an old army bush-jacket from which all the buttons had gone, and a *lungyi* which was not quite so brilliantly coloured as that worn by the boy who had brought their breakfast. Giving the same sign of obeisance the boy had used, the old man squatted on his haunches and looked at each of the three in turn, giving them a careful scrutiny.

Then, as if he had decided Hooky was the leader, he turned to him and in surprisingly good English said:

"*Thakin* (Sir), will you tell me something? Are you deserters from the British army?"

"Deserters!" Hooky roared, then looked round guiltily, half-afraid that his shout might have given away their hiding place.

Before he could recover the old man gave a little smile and nodded.

"So, you are not deserters," he said. "I saw you come here yesterday. I have a fish trap nearby, and from where that is, I can see the bridge. I heard the roar when the bridge was blown up—and my heart was warm. I do not love *Japani* men."

Hooky cleared his throat. He was not quite sure how he should address the old man, but suddenly remembering what the boy had said when he brought the food, decided on "headman" as being respectful.

"Headman, er . . . we're very grateful for the food last night. We were starving."

"No need to waste time thanking me, *Thakin*," the old man said gently. "I come here with bad news. *Japani* men have been to my village."

"Oh, strike a light!" Hooky groaned. "Are they near here?"

"*Japani* soldier not come here," the old man hastened to assure Hooky. "He come to my village for guide. Do you know that Thankyi bridge has been broken by the

British? There is great fighting at bridge. *Japani* army is held up. Masters of *Japani* army are angry."

"I'm not going to shed any tears over that," Hooky said.

"*Thakin*," the old Burmese said gently. "The *Japani* soldiers have taken one of my young men. He is to guide them through the jungle to another bridge. Maybe that will not be destroyed. If *Japani* army reaches that bridge . . . then their soldiers will fall on tired British army from rear. That would be bad!"

"Bad!" Jimmy Leach whispered, his eyes round as saucers. "It'd be the end. Where is this bridge?"

The old man smiled and nodded as if he approved.

"When the sun sets I shall send grandson for you. I will find guide to take you to bridge. If you get there before *Japani* men . . . you will destroy bridge, eh?" and his eyes gleamed. "I go now, in case *Japani* officer asks where I am. Rest, for there is much jungle country to cross if you would get to bridge in time." He rose, gave them another obeisance, then melted into the bushes and was gone.

For several minutes there was a stunned silence among the three, then Jimmy said:

"We'll never get there before the Japs. He admits they've taken a guide. That means they'll have a day's start on us. In any case, how can we bust a bridge without gear? We've no guncotton. We haven't a thing."

"We've got to do it, though," Hooky said soberly. "The old boy thinks we can, anyway, and I'd hate to let him down. I'm going to get some shut-eye. If we're going to be on nightwork . . . we don't want to be tired, eh, Banji?" and he turned to the Indian to give him an owl-like wink.

Bannerjee scratched idly at a fly on his neck and shruggèd. He could not understand this great hulking British soldier. He talked of beating the tireless Japanese soldiers to a distant bridge as if it really could be done. Bannerjee turned to Jimmy Leach who was idly cleaning his finger nails with the point of his army jack-knife.

Jimmy shrugged, spread his hands in a helpless gesture, then said:

"Don't ask me; leave it to Hooky. I'm going to try and sleep."

Half an hour after sunset the little Burmese boy re-appeared, and beckoned them to follow him.

5. Bridge over the Chindwin

QUARTER OF AN HOUR later they stood in a small clearing, lit by the tiniest of tiny lamps, staring dubiously at two elephants. The headman who had visited the trio that morning was waiting, his face grave as he *salaamed*.

"My young man who was to guide you has been forced to go with more *Japani* soldiers," he said quietly. "I have only grandson."

"Okay, if he knows the way," Hooky said, looking at the slim youngster, and then at the massive forms of the two elephants.

"Isn't it going to be too dangerous for him?" Jimmy Leach suggested. "He's only a boy, isn't he?"

"Better he die striking at *Japani* soldier than of starvation," was the quick retort. "And you must hurry. Several motor cars have gone through—the *Japani* officer with them took my son, who was to have been your guide. You will have to hurry to get to Chindwin bridge before them."

"*Hmit! Hmit!*" At the command to kneel both elephants obeyed, at which Hooky's eyes bulged. He had once ridden on an elephant when a very small boy, but that had been in a zoo, then a keeper had placed a short ladder against the huge beast so that passengers could clamber up.

Hooky was to sit behind the small boy whose name was Paw Tok. Jimmy Leach and Bannerjee would sit on the second elephant. A few moments later the huge beasts rose, and Hooky had to make a sudden grab at the boy sitting in front of him. Then began a nightmare journey.

With the youngster tickling behind the ears of his elephant with his toes, to make it turn one way or the other when they came to a fork in the narrow trail, they made their way into what by daylight must have seemed an impenetrable tract of jungle. They were following a wild elephant trail, and several times in the first half-hour Hooky was almost swept off the elephant's back by branches which spread across the trail.

Their mounts began to climb, and soon the moon was breaking through the thinning trees. They were crossing a range of hills, and Hooky Walker, who was said to have nerves of steel, went cold with horror at times when he looked to the right. The hill rose steeply on the left and dropped away for almost a thousand feet on the right. One slip would have sent the four-ton elephant and its human burden down to a horrible death in the trees and bamboo thickets below.

Bannerjee was more accustomed to this kind of thing than either Britisher, for his work with the Burma Teak Company had taken him into the wilder parts of Burma on a number of occasions and he had ridden elephants before.

Hour after hour the trek continued. They crossed two ranges of hills, then stopped to let the elephants rest and feed. Hooky was glad to get off the elephant, but afraid the delay might lose them the race to the bridge.

"Tell the youngster we must get cracking," he urged Bannerjee. The Indian spoke to the boy, then turned and with a resigned shrug explained:

"No use moving, sahib, until elephants rest. Boy says if we go on, elephants will stop later and then refuse to go on."

Hooky and Jimmy Leach watched the moon. It seemed to be racing across the sky, and the further it went the nearer was the dawn.

Two more ridges were crossed. Then, with the first pale fingers of the false dawn beginning to show in the east, they started to drop down the last hill. The boy had told them they were almost at the bridge, but Hooky had already caught a glimpse of a ribbon of silver—— the Chindwin River. Across that river ran the all-important bridge. If the Japs got it, then they could rush troops over and cut the British and Indian army's escape route.

It was when they were less than three hundred feet from the road leading to the bridge that they saw lights below. One—two—three pairs of headlights! The beams which jiggled up and down showed that it was a very poor road; but the Jap advance unit was pressing on. If they could get astride the Chindwin River, they would fight to the last man to protect it until the infantry, making a forced march behind them, came up.

Hooky called a halt. Bannerjee questioned the young Burmese boy, and got the answer that the bridge was about a mile away. They could keep on the hillside almost to the riverside itself.

"That's what we'll do," Hooky decided. "Banji, tell this laddie we've got to get down to the bridge quiet as if we were mice wearing woollen socks."

"Mice, sahib?" Bannerjee did not understand Hooky's humour.

"Forget it," Hooky snapped. "Tell him we've got to get down to the bridge quietly. If the elephants can't take us down . . . we'll dismount up the hill and do the rest on foot."

"Yes, sahib."

They skirted along the side of the hill, and sometimes the elephant on which Hooky was riding had to force its way through tangled undergrowth. To the Britisher's ears, the noise it made was so terrific that it seemed impossible that the sounds would go unheard.

Yet when they came out into a small clearing about a hundred feet above the river, the Japanese soldiers had not, apparently, heard their approach. Nearby and now stationary, stood the three vehicles which had enabled the advance unit to win the race to the bridge. In the grey light of dawn they could see that some of the slovenly looking sons of Nippon were cooking breakfast.

The remainder had crossed the river and set up machine-gun posts to prevent any British attempt to sabotage the way across. Hooky and the Burmese boy slid off their elephant. Bannerjee and Jimmy Leach followed their example.

"A couple of tommy-guns, and we could grab this end of the bridge," Jimmy said bitterly.

"Well, we've got this," Hooky said, swinging the Japanese revolver round with his right finger in the trigger guard. "Though we won't get far with this flippin' armament.

If we had just one tank ... even a little 'un, we'd sweep that riff-raff into ..."

"Sahib, sahib," there was sudden suppressed excitement in Bannerjee's voice. He grabbed Hooky by the arm and pointing to the elephants, whose large grey bodies merged into the gloom of the trees, went on: "The elephants."

"Eh?" For once Hooky just gaped.

"Long ago, sahib, elephants were used by Indian Rajahs in battle. They were fitted with metal shields on their foreheads, and employed to batter down city walls. If ..."

"Strike a light and stone the crows!" Hooky whispered, and now his eyes were shining. "Ask the kid if the elephants would go in ... against firing."

The boy frowned, then nodded. Even his short acquaintance with the Japanese had made him hate them. There followed a short council of war, with Bannerjee interpreting for the boy who understood only a word or so of English.

"It's got to be quick," Hooky insisted. "Don't forget, we've one flipping round of ammo. One, and one only! I'll go in behind the elephant. We've got to grab one of the machine-guns. I'll see to that. You grab rifles if you can."

"Are we letting the kid go in?" Jimmy Leach asked. "I mean . . . suppose he was killed. We can't send a kid in, can we?"

"Ask him if one of his elephants would go in alone," Hooky told Bannerjee, and got a firm headshake in reply. "Okay, tell him the Japs will be firing . . . unless we really can surprise them. He might be shot. I'm not going to force any kid to risk that."

The young Burmese smiled and touched a tiny object hanging from his neck by a thin silver chain. It was a charm, and young Paw Tok was convinced that as long as he wore the charm no bullet could harm him.

"I should have been wearing one of those," Jimmy Leach murmured, feeling at the bandage still round his head. If he turned his head quickly the bullet crease at the base of his skull still gave him a searing shock pain.

Paw Tok tethered one elephant by its hind

feet to a stout tree, then led the other down through the trees. They waited from a vantage point until they saw the soldiers gather about the cooking fire. The morning rice was heated up and tins of meat or fish had been opened.

Then one of the most desperate and forlorn charges of the Burma campaign began. Paw Tok *salaamed* to Hooky, *salaamed* to Jimmy and Bannerjee, then at a command from him the elephant curled the end of its trunk. The young Burmese put one brown foot in the trunk loop and was hoisted easily into position on the elephant's neck.

For such a huge beast the elephant moved with amazing quietness. It actually came out on to the dirt road within twenty yards of the Japanese before any of them saw it. Paw Tok was crouching down on the elephant's neck, and was probably never seen. Scratching behind the elephant's ears with his big toes, Paw Tok goaded his steed into a charge.

The Japs rose, hardly knowing what to do. Each man had his tin bowl of steaming rice and was loathe to drop it. An officer dragged out a revolver and fired two shots in quick succession at the charging elephant. It was the worst thing he could have done.

With a trumpet blast of rage which completed the demoralisation of the Japanese, the elephant increased its speed. It seemed to shuffle along, but was in fact doing about twenty miles an hour.

The khaki-clad soldiers scattered. The officer, with a courage which might have turned the tide had his revolver fired a heavier bullet, stood his ground and tried to stop the charging elephant. He died seconds later.

Then Hooky and his two friends came out of cover. Hooky had one thing on his mind then: to grab a machine-gun. Jimmy and Bannerjee were looking for rifles. In their panic-stricken rush only one of the Japanese had given a thought to the stacked weapons. He was a bespectacled N.C.O.

His belated rush for a weapon brought him the biggest headache he had ever known. Hooky Walker had boxed for the army. He was no brilliant boxer, but he had a punch which had earned him a string of one-round knock-outs. They might have brought him fame had there not been a war on.

His left hook caught the Jap N.C.O. on the side of the head, and as the man began to reel away, Hooky's right fist took him on the jaw. That N.C.O. was lucky, for he went out like a snuffed light, and missed the blast of machine-gun fire which downed the rest of his companions in the next few seconds.

Hooky swung the nearest machine-gun round, bellowed a warning to Jimmy Leach and Bannerjee, then opened up with a burst of fire which swept down the remainder of the fleeing crowd like grass before a well-swung scythe.

A few moments later Paw Tok's elephant died. The twelve men on the far side of the bridge, manning four machine-guns, and waiting patiently for their breakfast, heard the commotion and swinging one weapon round, poured a withering blast of fire across the bridge.

With a crash which made the ground tremble the huge grey-black beast swung

The officer fired two shots at the charging elephant.

round and crashed on to its side, dead before it hit the ground. Paw Tok was thrown clear and lay where he had fallen.

Hooky dropped face down, an action copied at once by Jimmy and Bannerjee. Hooky watched the bridge, while his two friends faced the other way, just in case any of the detachment had escaped the first blast of fire from Hooky's captured *Nambu* machine-gun.

"Tac-tac-tacatacacacacacacacaca!" A second Jap machine-gun opened up, and the air hummed with the small-calibre bullets. Hooky edged backwards out of the line of fire, dragging his weapon with him. The bridge was a well-made one, with stout wooden rails, and these offered some protection, though bullets raked the wood and filled the air with flying splinters.

"I can hold this lot," Hooky bawled. "Get the boy out of the way. Behind the elephant if you can. That'll act as a shield."

Jimmy crawled slowly towards Paw Tok, and finally got him behind the bulky shape of the dead elephant. After a minute or so the bursts of machine-gun fire from the other side of the bridge slackened. One gun was kept in action with short bursts to discourage the unknown attackers. Finally even that gun stopped.

" What do we do now?" Jimmy asked. " The youngster is coming round. I think he got a thump on the head when he was thrown off the elephant."

Hooky scratched his mop of dust-filled hair.

" Whatever we do, we've got to do it quick," he decided. " The Jap footsloggers can't be so far behind. Once they arrive— that's it. I'm trying to think what we can do to knock this flippin' bridge down. It's wood, but it looks solid."

" We could burn it down," Jimmy suggested. " The timber should be bone-dry."

" Got a bit of paper to start the fire?" Hooky asked sarcastically. " I'd thought of burning, but you won't do any Boy Scout two-matches-to-start-a-fire trick on this little lot."

" Petrol, sahib," the suggestion came from Bannerjee. " There will be plenty in the car tanks."

"You've got something there," Hooky agreed. "Come across here, Jimmy, and keep your hands on this machine-gun. I'll check the nearest car."

"Don't be daft," said Jimmy angrily. "I've forgotten more about cars than you ever knew."

"Okay, okay, but make it quick. I've got a feeling we can't waste time."

A hot, sticky silence fell over the scene. The Japanese on the other bank were content to wait. They knew their infantry could not be far away, and once they came up, the fate of this little group—stragglers left behind by the retreating British—would be sealed.

"Tank's half-full," Jimmy reported. "I could swing it round, start it going across the bridge, then we could shoot into the petrol tank."

"And run up with a match?" Danger had sharpened Hooky's thinking powers, so that he was seeing snags much quicker than was usual. "See if there's anything in the car we could use as a sort of fuse. A piece of rope, or something, you could soak in oil."

While Jimmy was looking in the car's tool-kit young Paw Tok got to his feet and staggered towards the trees. His movement brought a burst of machine-gun fire, but the boy had sense enough to throw himself flat, and escaped uninjured. Then he crawled into the trees.

To Bannerjee's question as to where he was going, Paw Tok, a sob in his voice, said he was going to see if his other elephant was safe.

"Poor little tick," Hooky said. "I reckon losin' an elephant is worse'n losing your pet dog."

Jimmy Leach was unravelling a piece of rope, preparatory to soaking it in petrol when Paw Tok re-appeared among the trees. His shout made Bannerjee's eyes widen with sudden fear.

"Sahib," he called urgently to Hooky. "The boy says he can see marching men round the bend of the road. The *Japani* foot soldiers are coming."

"Get that car moving, Jimmy," Hooky bawled. "Or it'll be too late."

For once Jimmy Leach refused to be hurried.

"You do your job and I'll do mine," he yelled back and continued soaking the length of unravelled rope he had found in the car's tool-kit. Then he tied it to the back of the car, trailed the rope out to its end—some ten feet away, and striking a match, applied the flame.

"Give me some covering fire, Hooky," he yelled, and jumping into the driving seat slammed into first gear then lifted his foot off the clutch pedal. The car jerked forward even as Hooky sent a withering blast of machine-gun fire along the length of the bridge. The bullets kicked up dust, and sent splinters flying from the floorboards of the bridge. He lifted his sights a little and three men who had just dragged a machine-gun into the open at the other end of the bridge fell over backwards, and did not get up.

Jimmy drove the car on to the end of the bridge, then leaped out. He rushed round the back of the car and pushed with every ounce of strength he could muster. It just saved the engine from stalling. Then at a slow walking pace it rolled on to the bridge, and as Jimmy raced off and dived for cover, more Japanese appeared at the other end, and opened up. A bullet sliced the heel of Jimmy's right boot, and the impact flung him full length.

He rolled over and over to get out of the field of fire, and as he did so he heard Paw Tok screaming something from the trees. Bannerjee interpreted the Burmese boy's words. The Japs were less than two hundred yards away, and hearing the firing had broken into a trot.

"Bust the petrol tank," Jimmy gasped.

"You teach your grandmother how to suck eggs," Hooky grunted, and aiming at the back of the slowly moving car, squeezed the trigger.

"Tac-a-tac-a-tac-atac-a-tac!" It was only a short burst, but it was enough to puncture the armoured cover of the petrol tank. Petrol spurted out of the back of the car and it burst into flames.

From the far side of the bridge men began to shout. The rattle of the machine-gun stopped, and four Japanese began to race towards the burning car. Behind them three others appeared. No matter what anyone said about the Japanese soldier, he was brave and fanatical in his desire to serve his Emperor.

Realising what the appearance of the car on the bridge meant, especially now that it had burst into flames, they were racing across in the hope of being able either to push it back off the bridge, or maybe even topple it over the low rails into the river below.

Hooky stopped them. Had there been anyone in authority to watch him, Hooky Walker might well have joined the ranks of men who can put the letters V.C. behind their names.

Lifting the Japanese light machine-gun he hurried on to the bridge. The gun sprayed lead, the shuddering recoil made Hooky jerk like a man with the palsy; but he never stopped. An officer on the far side of the blazing vehicle seeing his men fall, whipped out his revolver, took aim, and fell riddled with bullets before he could fire.

"Come on, you clowns," Hooky roared. "I'm not coming back."

Then, and only then, did Jimmy Leach and Bannerjee rush on to the bridge. Behind them, the first few just appearing round the bend in the dusty road, came half a dozen Japanese infantrymen.

The first man stopped, dropped to one knee, and cocking his rifle fired; but there was nothing to see save a growing cloud of oily smoke. The petrol from the punctured tank was pouring out, and oily flames were spreading across the bridge like water from a tap.

There were dead and dying Japanese on the bridge as Hooky marched out, the gun still spitting death. Nor did he stop until the trailing ammunition belt had been jerked spasmodically through the gun and the last round of ammunition had been fired. He threw the gun over the bridge parapet and sprinted the last dozen yards to the far bank.

As he did so there was a bellowing roar as the car petrol tank exploded.

From the shelter of the jungle-covered hillside on the north bank of the Chindwin, Hooky, Jimmy Leach and Bannerjee watched the fire. The Japanese fought like madmen to save the bridge; they had marched with little rest through the night, and the only utensils they had for carrying water were their rice bowls. To make matters worse for them the river was seventy feet below, for here it ran through a gorge.

At the end of an hour the first blazing timbers began to drop into the river, and the flames roared unchecked all the way along the sun-dried timbering. This way across the Chindwin river was closed to the Japanese army, for some days at least.

When they were out of sight of the troops on the opposite bank Hooky, Jimmy Leach and Bannerjee came out of the trees and struck west along the dirt road. They were tired and hungry, but feeling on top of the world; but a mile from the bridge they were halted in their tracks when a muffled voice from some bushes snarled:

"You shower of ticks. If I'd been a Jap gunner you'd all be dead now. Where do you think you . . ." then the voice trailed off, and a goggle-eyed Sergeant Morris stepped out on to the road.

"Sarge!" Hooky roared. "What a flippin' sight for sore eyes. Got a fag?"

"Sergeant!" The exasperated voice of Captain Johnson stopped Morris just as he was feeling in his bush-jacket for a crumpled packet of cigarettes. "Come on, it's fixed."

Hooky, Jimmy and Bannerjee trotted after Sergeant Morris. They pulled up as a battered, dust-covered Scout car backed out of a small clearing at the side of the jungle where it had been pushed when the engine broke down. Sergeant Morris had been sent ahead to give warning of the approach of any enemy. Captain Johnson and Harrison had stayed to fix the engine.

At sight of the trio, Captain Johnson stood up.

"Walker and Leach!" he croaked. "You

can't kill 'em, can you, Sergeant? Who's the other man."

"*Jemadar* Bannerjee, sir, Burma Rifle Brigade," Jimmy Leach said, stiffening to attention. "We picked him up near the other bridge. . . ."

"All right, you can tell me later," Captain Johnson interrupted. "We've a job to do. Have you come across the Chindwin Bridge? Did you see any sign of the Japs?"

"Hundreds of 'em sir," Hooky said gleefully, and even as Captain Johnson winced, thinking he was too late to stop the Japs crossing, Hooky went on: "But they'll not worry you. The bridge is down . . . or nearly down. We set it on fire."

Ordering the tired trio to stay where they were, Captain Johnson drove the Scout car along to the bridge to make sure. When he drove back he stepped out on to the dusty road and did something he had never done before. He brought out his cigarette case, opened it, and offered Hooky, Jimmy and Bannerjee a smoke.

"I don't know how you did it," he said, offering them a light, for not one of the trio had a serviceable box of matches, "but the thing is flaming like a torch."

"Sahib," Bannerjee said, saluting, and then pointing to Hooky. "He is hero. He saved us. He should be mentioned in despatches," and fumbling at the little cluster of bronze oak leaves which Hooky had pinned on him earlier, he undid the decoration and holding it out to an amused Captain Johnson said: "Sir, respectfully beg you decorate him on field of battle."

"We don't do things that way, *Jemadar*," Captain Johnson said, chuckling, "But I'll bear it in mind. In the meantime, get in the car. Even if the engine doesn't break down we're going to be the last out of Burma. Start her up, Harrison."